Greater Sampson County Swamp Sheep Hunt

Greater Sampson County Swamp Sheep Hunt

Bobby Rupert

ISBN 978-1-300-18606-9

My life has been full of good bird dogs, good friends, and good hunting. These stories evolved from these times and are part of my memoirs.

–Bobby

Dedication

This book is dedicated to my parents who helped me unselfishly to develop my love of Southern life, heritage, and the outdoors.

And to my wife who has spent countless nights cleaning up after wild puppies and mending clothes and things from their onslaught.

To my children and grandchildren for whom this book was written, so that hopefully you can gain some insight into the way my generation grew up and how our life circled around work, church, and family. Our pride in country was unwavering and our president and other officials were held in the highest regard. I have always looked out for the land, water, and resources, and I pray your generation can understand this value and protect our resources. I fear that the more disenfranchised from the land each generation becomes, the less they will understand its importance.

And off course to all the canines that have had such an impact on me:

Arno, Sparky, Bo, Duke, and Kirk (pre- college).

Boy, Bell, Judy, Zack, Blue, and Zip (bird dogs).

David O, Sidney, Cotton, Split, Red, Shag, Tiger Scruffy, Jeb, and off course, Gus.

Rarely in your life do you get to cooperate with a great dog, I mean a truly special and gifted dog. I have owned hundreds of dogs, and so many were special in so many ways, but there has always been a place in my heart reserved for that really special dog.

Gus (Golden Gus) was such a dog. Always a great friend, he was all business in the field, and everyone that ever hunted with him was vested with lifelong memories. He hunted with stars, politicians, and just regular people. He hunted with field champions as well as dogs not so well known. It didn't matter what kind of bird we were hunting, Gus knew what to do. He lived to hunt!

Golden Gus

Acknowledgements

I never would have had the opportunity to live this book if it was not for all the great dogs that God has put in my path or all the great men I was able to share them with. J.K. prodded me to write the book and gave unselfish feedback. The competitive spirit of Anson made me a better shot, and the preciseness of Bruce a better hunter. We have spent many hours in the field, and I cherished every minute. The Golden Gus accompanied me on most of my hunts for twelve years. We shared many field lunches and great hunts mostly due to his efforts. I trained a lot of dogs since you left, old friend, but none had your ability. I thank God for all my bountiful blessings.

Prologue

This book is based on the many people and dogs I have had the privilege to meet in my many decades in the field. I was fortunate to have some money at a young age and used it to develop my love of hunting, fishing, and dogs. I started the Pamlico Manor Hunting Lodge in Hyde County, North Carolina in the mid-1980s, and from there I was able to guide hunters all over our great country and some international sites as well. Most of these stories originated from this period of my life, and be assured no fact or situation was held firm when an embellishment made the stories better. The stories are all fiction, but most have more than a grain of truth.

Table of Contents

Greater Sampson County Swamp Sheep Hunt

As I pulled into the driveway of the Pamlico Manor Lodge, the ole pickup's brake rotors were squealing and the truck was sliding on the fresh layer of sleet gathering on the blacktop. It was as cold as a bear's butt, and I was tired, cold, and hungry from being out on the sound all day duck hunting. I just wanted to go in and have a drink or two, sit by the fire, and warm up. But after I slid into my parking space and walked through the lodge doors, I was hit smack in the face with the loudest, most boisterous ruckus I'd ever encountered in the lodge. I looked around to see what was making such a fuss and there they stood—two snowbirds (Yankees): George and Stanley Steinbeck from New York.

George was a bear of a man, and he was big and hairy and even louder than a four-stand band. Stanley was the opposite of George, a slight sort of guy with beady eyes and a shifty look and sharp nose. Both of them looked like they were dressed from a Filson catalog, without a stain or tear on anything they wore—heck, even their boots were shiny. And they were drinking and eating and just having one helluva good time. They were so out of place they looked like a pair of flat-footed chickens in a coyote race just waiting to be plucked.

Well, I saw green—I mean money—so I got in there and started to talk to them; we shucked oysters and ate shrimp and had a few drinks. I encouraged the conversation and kept pouring them Plum-Bob, which was shine that had wild plum and sugar in the jar. We procured this high-quality nectar from a secret location in Johnston County, and I was using it to loosen their tongues. They got to telling me how they were world-class hunters. They'd been all over the world collecting trophies and they'd chosen our Pamlico Manor Lodge to come and kill a trophy black bear for their trophy rooms. Well, Hyde County in them days had had a big moratorium on black bears for a lot of years, and this was the first year they had open hunting on bear in quite a few seasons. Some writer in one of them fancy magazines had written an article on black bears of Hyde County, and they'd read about us in that magazine and how there was a good chance to kill a record bear here, and they wanted to kill a big black bear bad.

So we had lots of conversation on what they wanted to kill and got the bear plans all worked out. George said he wanted to kill a big one—over five hundred pounds. Now at that time Hyde County did not have a kill on record of a five-hundred-pound bear, but tale was there were some, at least George thought so. I asked them if they had their guns, and if they wanted to zero them in, and if everything was ready to go hunting first thing in the morning, and they confirmed all their gear was in good shape and ready to go.

So the next morning I got them up at 5:00 a.m. to have breakfast, and here came Stanley Steinbeck with his gun in one hand and a scope in the other, both brand new, right out of a box. He said, "How do you put this thing on? It's not like my other one." I could see right off that he did not have any scope rings, or mounts…I mean he had nothing to put that scope on that gun. I immediately started to have some pretty big doubts about my "world-class hunters": now I wasn't saying Stanley was slow, but his five o'clock shadow didn't show until around 7:30. Anyway, I explained to them that we didn't have the equipment—we weren't a gun shop, and we couldn't fix his rifle this morning, but we could loan him a rifle. So we put him in a rifle a big Wheatherby 300 magnum zeroed at two hundred yards, where he could hold on target from point blank to three hundred yards, and I put Stanley in the truck and took George out and gave him to Oberg, one of the best big game guides who took George out to his truck. We arrived at our hunting area and I put Stanley in his stand and gave him instructions to help his hunt. I gave him information about the wind direction and where the feed plots were located. I told him if he shot a bear for safety not to leave his stand until I was back, and we would approach the kill together. Then I left him as I went to take care of some other things and help some other hunters; as I left, I yelled over my shoulder that I would be back about two hours later.

Now I was heading out on sixth avenue on Lux Farm, on my way back to the lodge. I went the long way to check on some other hunters, and after I had gone about a mile, I could see movement way down the road, and low and behold it was George Steinbeck running down the road without a rifle, without nothing at all, waving his arms and jumping up and down, yelling "There's a bear, there's a bear over there!" I mean that bear had scared the living crap outa him. The best I could tell was that a bear had come out of the brush and leaned on George's stand to rest and maybe scratch his back. This startled George, and he broke and ran from his stand, leaving his gun and shooting bag. When I found George he was winded and sweaty and had torn those new Filson pants and picked the crap out of his sweater on some bamboo briars—he had cuts and scratches on his hands, neck, and face where he had run through those briars. I got George rounded up and calmed down, and when I opened the truck door, he literally sailed into the truck like a Wood Duck hen flying into a duck box at sixty miles per hour, just stopping before she breaks her neck on the other side. He looked scared and was pale and clammy like he was ready to puke, so we drove the truck back to his stand and recouped his rifle and gear.

Now that I had George and he had gotten a hold of himself, I rode him around a little bit to see if we could find anything moving, and we finally found a bear out there feeding at the edge of a cut. I rolled down the window on George's side and helped him find the bear in the cut. He jacked a round in his rifle but short shucked the bolt so he had a jam, which we soon cleared. He was hyperventilating and shaking and sweating like a tush hog, but I finally steadied him by getting him to take deep breaths. He was moving the rifle barrel badly, and somehow when he shot, he hit the bear solid, and managed to kill about a three-hundred-pound black bear.

Well, that night back at the Manor, everybody was drinking liquor and having a big time, farting, scratching, and grunting, and generally doing all things hunters do when they're away from home. Now that we were back to safety, George had forgotten his morning fright, and he and Stanley were again bragging about all the trophies they had killed all over the world, like shooting a gazelles at a full run at four hundred yards from a moving truck, and hitting Kudu in the eye at two hundred yards in thick bush because that was all they could see. From all this talk I knew they were full of baloney: I decided that George was slicker than a Nutria Rat's belly sliding down a mud levee, and I was going to try and pick me some snowbirds.

So I started to bait them a little, and said "You know a bear's a fine trophy, and a lion's a majestic kill, but the greatest trophy anyone can ever have is a swamp sheep—matter of fact, I heard John Wayne had one in his trophy room."

Boy, their ears perked up just like radar. "What do you mean a swamp sheep?" I said, "Well, when Desoto and his gang come through our country hundreds of years ago, they had some country sheep with them for food, now some of those sheep got loose and went wild, and they run the swamps around here still today. Everybody around here knows of them, but few have ever killed one; some have seen one and most outdoorsmen here have smelled one cause they stink worse than the garlic breath of an Italian pizza maker, or downwind of a road-killed pole cat. They have a great big set of horns that sweep backwards with shiny ivory tips and a long flowing mane on their chest sort of like a lion. Today's your lucky day because the best ones are the Sampson county swamp sheep, and I happen to own a farm right smack in the center of their prime habitat, Mingo Swamp, Sampson County. My place is right on the Little Juniper Creek, dead center of trophy swamp sheep habitat—everyone knows Juniper creek sheep are heavier and their horns are bigger.

Now this really got George and Stanley's attention, and they wanted to go first thing in the morning, but I had to inform them that the sheep were not here in Hyde County, but over in Sampson County where I come from, about a hundred miles west of here. I told George and Stanley that it's almost impossible to get a tag to shoot one, but I know the governor, and since you all are very distinguished Barristers from New York City, maybe I can get you a special permit, but it's expensive, I mean expensive as the dickens to get a permit to shoot swamp sheep, and I doubt you can afford it. "Well, how much is it? We can pay, we got money." Now that I had the boys lathered up, all I needed to do was shave them, so I said, "It'll cost you $5,000 a piece to go, and if we kill one you gotta pay a trophy fee of $2,500." Well, they wanted to do it, because they had never been on a swamp sheep hunt and nobody they knew had ever been on a swamp sheep hunt and they wanted this rare trophy for their trophy room. But what they didn't know was that I had never been on a swamp sheep hunt and had never seen a swamp sheep, and to my knowledge there were not any wild sheep of any kind in Sampson County. But that was ok because I had a plan.

Anyhow, they finished up the bear hunt the next day, and we made a plan for them to come to Sampson County for sheep hunting two weeks later. They'd come to Raleigh, where I'd pick them up and put them up in a hotel, and then we'd get them out for a swamp sheep hunt. Now I'd had some exotic animals down there under high fence in Hyde County, like that Axis Deer, Fallow Deer, Sitka Deer, and some Aoudad Sheep and Mouflon Sheep too. I thought I'd catch me one of them Aoudad Sheep as they are sort of big and ugly looking, and take them to Sampson County and run them through the swamp, so the boys could get a shot at one. So I made a deal with Oberg to put two of them Aoudad sheep in our stock trailer; then I gave him specific instructions on what to do after he had driven the sheep to Dunn. I said, "Now Oberg, at 7:30 in the morning, drive the horse trailer down the field right here at the back cut of the woods where the path goes through the big stand of poplars, and you back up into that path to let that sheep out of the trailer. Back the trailer right down the trail and open the gate—if you stick him in the butt with a hot shot, he'll take off running, and I think he'll run right down that trail." Oberg said, "You mean you want to juice him on the ass with that electric stick? That's brutal." I said, "Yes, burn his butt and get him running and hollering and snorting and slobbering real good." I had built a nice blind about a hundred yards down that trail, and I thought the sheep would come our way as they were tame pasture sheep—I didn't think they would run through the briars and thickets—I figured the sheep would run along that trail down by us, and we could get a shot. I said "Now Oberg, after you let out the first one, don't do nothing, just wait, wait in the truck about an hour and then send out the other sheep the same way." We had it all planned out.

Well, I had my two snowbirds out there early that morning, and they were excited. We were brushing us up a blind so that they could work up a lather as well as work off some energy so that their hunt would not end too quickly and they wouldn't have the chance to feel unrewarded for accomplishing too little. We got the end of the blind opened up some so that they could stick out a rifle and shotgun, and we opened up some firing lanes. We sat there and watched the sun come up, and about 7:10 in the morning, I put my coffee down and I sniffed the air and said "I can smell him—can you smell him?" This got the boys excited, and they were breathing hard, trying hard to make scent, and could not sit still on their stools. Well, you could hear a little traffic going up and down on Highway 421 where we were, and they couldn't distinguish that traffic from the truck and trailer coming on the backside of the woods. I could hear Oberg coming with the trailer, and I heard the horse trailer tailgate squeak just a little bit. And then I heard a baahhhhhh, and I knew he had done put the hot shot in that boy's tail. I said "Ya'll get ready, there'll be one coming soon, I can smell him good." They all hunkered down there, and we looked like Davy Crocket at the Alamo with the rifles hanging over the side waiting for them swamp sheep to come by.

About that time we heard a tear and a ruckus, and around the curve here he comes, "a Greater Sampson County Swamp Sheep." What a site to behold with them long curved back horns, long mane on his breast, his nose flared, and long strings of slobber everywhere. Well with George being the older of the two brothers, he decided he was in charge, and he claimed rank to be the first one to get a shot. So he throwed his rifle up there and the sheep walked right up the path toward the blind and stopped about eighty yards across from the blind and stood there broadside, and I heard: Kaboom! Kaboom! Kaboom! He hit him one time in the back hindquarters and once on the front leg but did not knock him down. Lord, I didn't want that sheep to get away—that was money! Besides I didn't want to trek through the Mingo Swamp all day looking for a Greater Sampson County Swamp Sheep. So I said "Well, we'd better finish him off," and I handed him a shotgun; he shot him three more times and finally killed him. So I went out there and hung a tag on him that I had gotten from Piedmont Airlines, and we congratulated each other for such a great hunt. We whooped and hollered and had just the biggest time celebrating the great hunting skills of George Steinbeck. Finally I said we'd better get back in the blind and be quiet if we wanted a chance to get Stanley a sheep—I told them that Swamp Sheep have been known to travel about nine or ten o'clock to their bedding grounds, and we might get another one if we were really, really lucky. So we got back in the blind and I got Stanley ready for a shot.

The sun had warmed things up by then, and as we sat there, I got sleepy and drifted back in time and could hear Grandpa talking about how nobody was as dumb as a snowbird; in fact they were the only people in the world that would pay to see alligator wrestling, and as I sat there in my own memories I heard the squeak of the horse trailer gate that brought me back to the present, and I said "Boys, I can smell another one, can you smell him coming from the east? Now them boys did not know the difference between east and the direction to Mars, so I pointed and said there's another one coming out of the "swamp." Sure enough, about four or five minutes later, there he came, just trotting up the trail. Stanley was primed up, his knuckles white and his finger tight on the trigger; he was as tight as a coon in a forked branch after eating mulberries all night. Stanley commenced to shoot—I think he shot at him four times and didn't even hit him. He had that gun barrel waiving all over the place and bark flying from tree trunks and dirt flying, as he shot all his bullets, and that ole sheep just stood there—he didn't know where to go or what was going on, he just stood there looking, wondering if someone was going to bring him a pan of corn. Finally, Stanley calmed down and made a good shot; he finally killed him, and we celebrated by jumping and hollering "Great shot!" and such as that.

Well, the real work now started as we got those sheep up a pole and took at least a thousand pictures. I field dressed them on the spot and caped out the hide, then rolled the hides up in a tight roll while sprinkling salt between each layer, put the hides in a heavy cardboard box with the horns on top, and sent them to a high-powered taxidermist in Benson to be mounted. Everybody had had a great time, and we were slapping each other on the back, hugging each other and telling each other we were like brothers and how we would always keep in touch and hunt together. The brothers paid me and gave me a big tip to boot, plus Stanley gave me his Filson hat that I wore for many years until I lost it in a blizzard in North Dakota. As we loaded up and headed for the airport, those guys had a bigger grin that a possum eating corn and said they had never had a better hunt anywhere in the world.

Years have passed and I have never had another call, and I guess I will never see George and Stanley again, but I envision that somewhere in their office, in a big skyscraper in New York City, perhaps right up over their door, there are two great big mounted Greater Sampson County Swamp Sheep.

Big Red

Big Red

We all stood around the air crate looking in at the little, dark fur ball with white eyes sticking out, and I said, "Ain't she a pretty puppy?" I had bought a puppy off of Cy Cyfeers from Minnesota, and she was a Piper Pacer pup. Piper was a big-time Field Champion back in the 70s. We're talking about a Labrador Retriever for you greenhorns. I had shipped her home, and she was one pretty thing. I raised her and did her yard work, then sent her off to Ken Richardson to be trained. We worked her and worked her, and that little hussy was rolling. Before she was two years old and aged out, we were trying to get her on the derby list, and everything was going fine.

Her name was Katie, and it looked like she was gonna be a real big-time dog for me. Well, she was a slow bloomer, and just before she turned two, she had her first season, and it was one hot heat. Katie was always obedient, but now that she was in heat, she listened like a lot of women do: none at all. I let her out of the house one morning, and she took off running, and ran out of sight with me running behind her, blowing a whistle and hollering. The biggest insult of all was that this was only three days before dove season. Now when you lose your dog three days before dove season, just when they are supposed to be fetching all your dead birds and showing all the other hunters what a fine dog you have, that's tragic. But anyhow, I rode to the end of the farm and saw her and this great big ole red dog of nondescript breeding together. I thought oh great, now here we're gonna have some puppies that we don't want. Nonetheless I called and I called, but Katie never came up. They run off, her and that big red dog.

Well, I looked and looked, and three days later, that big ole red dog was in my yard, just sitting there without Katie. But he was real man shy, and he'd just scoot away if you came near him and wouldn't never let you touch him. From that day forward I had made it my quest to get a hold of the big red dog, I guess because he was our last link to Katie. To this day I have no idea what happened to her, if she was hit by a car, or if someone stole her or what. But that ole red dog stayed in my front yard day after day. He sat all the way out by the road. I'd try to coax him and after about a month he would get about forty feet from me. Every night I would sit on the porch and call him.

So one day I went to Freddie Tew's, our local grocery and gossip center, and bought me a sack of Bright Leaf, red hot hot dogs and took them back home. Now Bright Leaf is second only to Jack Mackeral for dog comfort food, but it's hard to chunk Jack Mackerel. When I got back home I went straight to the front porch eating Bright Leaf red hots (Carolina Style Sausage) and looking at Big Red, and while looking at him it became natural to start calling him Big Red so I throwed one out there for him and he wolfed her down. After about three weeks of daily red hot treatment, he was coming up to within two to three feet of me. Well, one day he comes up very close and I touched him on his nose. And when that happened, there was an instant transformation: he immediately became our dog. He became a wonderful, wonderful family dog. Stayed in the garage and guarded our house for twelve or more years before he died.

But ole Big Red was a legend around Green Path Road. Now Red had a terrible bad scar on his back right leg, like maybe he had been caught in a steel trap when he was young. He was bold and strong and if any stray dog in the community came by our house he'd run them off. But now if I brought in a new bird dog or a lab and brought them around him on a leash so he could get a good sniff, then he'd accept them and all would be ok. But Big Red had a tendency to get into trouble, and he loved his women sure enough, so every time I'd have a bitch come into season, he'd do everything he could to break the door down and get to the bitch. The majority of the time I was successful keeping him away, but every now and then his abilities and tenacity won out, and I'd have a bitch bred by Big Red.

During this time my wife had a little long-haired Jack Russell named Fluffy, just a little poo-poo sissy dog, but everywhere he went he thought he was sure enough a bad dog. Well, Big Red was there eating scraps one day and Fluffy came up and growled at him, and when he did, Big Red reached up and grabbed him. He wasn't even a good mouthful, and Big Red shook his head about three times and Fluffy was dead. Unfortunately, the children were there, and they saw it—it was terrible and tragic, and they took the little fluffy dog to the vet, but there won't nothing that could be done. My daughters and my wife were just mad as a wet setting hen. And they told me I had to do something about Big Red. Well, the definition of "doing something" meant getting rid of him or killing him or something harsh, cause he couldn't stay there anymore. So they stayed on me for a day, and I put ole Big Red in the truck and drove him to the back side of the farm. I let him out of the pickup, and he was sitting there on the ground, and I pulled my pistol out and pointed it to his head. And I said, "Big Red, I really like you, and I really hate to see you go, but the golden rule from the bible says an eye for an eye and a tooth for a tooth: you killed Fluffy, and now you have to pay the price."

I don't know exactly what happened next, but I heard a horn back up at the house, and maybe that rushed things, I don't know. But I cocked my pistol, pointed it at Big Red and shot him right in the head. Well, he fell over and then took off running and fell in the ditch. Meanwhile, I took off back up to the house—I didn't want whoever it was to be coming to the back of the farm in the middle of a dog killing. So I went up there and it was somebody there trying to borrow the pig cooker. So we talked, hooted, and hollered a minute, then hooked up their truck to the pig cooker, and they took off. So I went back down there to get Big Red and go bury him.

When I got back there to where he was, Big Red was gone. I couldn't find him anywhere. I looked and looked for him and finally found some blood spots leading back to the house. When I got back to the house there's my wife and daughters under the garage holding Big Red who is bleeding everywhere. "Don't shoot him, don't shoot him!" they hollered. Like I'm gonna shoot him under my garage with my children and wife holding him. Well, evidently that was a high enough fine to pay for Big Red, because they pardoned him on the spot. They let him inside and doctored him and then put him out there in the dog box under the garage. I figured his brain would swell up and he'd die, but old Big Red was tough; he laid there in that box where they'd hand feed him, and after about four or five days he started getting up and around a bit. Before long Big Red was well, and he'd run around there for another four or five years without any more incidents.

Until one day I had a champion bird dog out there in the yard, and before I knew it, Big Red had covered her and they were making puppies. I said, "Lord Red, I can't have this no more, it's expensive, and you're messing up my dogs. "I had promised Red I would not ever try to kill him again, but I had to do something. So I looked around in my vet stuff, and I found some rubber bands, and I banded his testicles (his balls); well about four or five or so days later, his balls fell off, and Big Red had become an "it."

It didn't seem to bother him aside from the fact that he gained a little more weight. He probably weighed 100 or 110 pounds at the time, so I thought everything was fine in life with Big Red. Well, one day about a week later, another bird dog bitch in heat was out in the yard, and Sue said, "Watch out, Big Red is out there and that bird dog is loose." I said, "Oh, don't worry about that. I fixed Big Red—he's a eunuch." What I didn't know is that there is a period of time after your testicles are gone that you are still making sperm, and Big Red was still potent. Well, he covered that bitch and he bred her—that's when he got the nickname Hero. As a matter of fact, we wrote a slogan for Red after that: Forever more, he will be our Hero. You can shoot him in the head and you can't kill him, you can cut his balls off and you can't keep him from breeding." But any rate, ole Big Red, he stayed around the house many more years. He was a very, very endearing dog, and we all loved him greatly. He was just a great, family dog. As he got older, he got heavier, and he waddled around looking a lot like Buddha, but every night when you got home, he was there under the garage to smile a at you, and he just wanted to be loved and make you feel welcomed. We loved Big Red.

As he aged, he went blind in one eye with cataracts; and he got real arthritic where he could hardly go; and he got to where he couldn't hear at all, I mean he couldn't hear a lick. I reckon it's deafness that did him in. The sad part of the story is Big Red would go across the street to the neighbor's every day, just like a clock. Our neighbors would throw their dinner scraps out in the yard, and Big Red would go help them clean them up. He was out there one day and was on his way back, waddling across the street, and he didn't see the hog truck coming. Now Big Red was a big dog and feared by most other dogs, but he won't no comparison to a hog truck—that Peterbuilt mashed him flat, killed him dead as a hammer. Well, I hate to tell you how sad we all were, tears in everybody's eyes. I took ole Big Red up to the place of honor where I have buried several special dogs. This was the same place I was gonna bury him the first time. I finally buried him with a tear running down my face, and I looked at him and said, "Big Red, you'll always be my hero."

Bobby, Boy and Betty

Betty

Back in the 70s I was hunting two ole dogs, one pointer and one setter. One was a big ole black-and-white belton setter named Boy, and he was one fine setter dog, and I had a little ole orange-and-white pointer bitch, Bell, and she was a mighty fine little bitch. The only problem was that neither one of them was as good a dead bird dog as I like to have. So I was looking through the The Raleigh News and Observer Sunday paper every week, looking in the want ads for a broke bird dog. After several weeks of searching, I found an ad that said "Broke Bird Dog for Sale." The dog was in Standfield, North Carolina, not far from Red Cross, So I called the man up—he was a preacher down there in Stanfield who trained and sold bird dogs on the side. I asked him about the dog in the ad, and he said, "I got a gype named Betty who's four years old, a liver-and-white bitch—she ain't much to look at, but she's a good bird dog." I said, "I don't expect she can keep up, because I got some pretty high-powered dogs, but if she's a good dead bird dog, and she backs well, she'll do what I need." He said, "She is a excellent dead bird dog, and she's back on site just like she is supposed to. And she's a good bird dog to boot." So I drove up to Stanfield, North Carolina in my wife's brand new white Monte Carlo with its green top, a '73 model.

We left Dunn about 4:00 a.m. as we had to be there early. Now my buddy Bruce and Charlie my college suite mate had ridden with me out there to see Mr. Furr—I believe that was his name. After we met and shook hands and talked a spell about bird dogs, democrats, and religion, he let Betty out of the pen. We put her in his old jeep and we took off, and as it was a Sunday morning, he had to hurry cause he had to get back to church to preach.

We went to a little ole place a cut over that he knew, a sort of rolling country compared to the flat lands where I come from. We let her out and she took off a hunting right then while we followed behind her. It won't long before she pointed. Well, she pointed and held without taking a single step until we flushed the birds, but didn't none of us have a gun, as it was Sunday. Truth is, I really didn't care to see how good of a bird dog she really was anyway—I was far more interested in seeing how good a dead bird dog she was. The Birds flushed wild and fanned outdown in the bottom of a draw, and we went down there behind them, but before we got to the bottom of the draw well, Betty pointed again, and she did a pretty good job. Just about that time I saw Mr. Furr start jumping around and saying "Pole cat!"

I had no idea of what was going on—we ain't got no pole cats in Sampson County and I didn't know what that was. For those of you that don't know, a pole cat's a skunk. When you're bird hunting, you really don't want to get personal with a skunk and you don't want your dog doing so either. But Betty had done sailed in on one and was a shaking and killing him. Mr. Furr took off running up the hill, and I turned around and started running with him, cause I didn't want to stay there with the dog and pole cat neither.

Well, Mr. Furr being a good Sunday preacher, he knew how to spin a tale and work with the word. We was running up that hill, and I looked behind me, and he took to running faster, and I caught another gear to keep up with him. He said "Bo, you see that dog right there?" I said "Yeah." He said "Well, don't you see what's in her mouth?" I said, "Yeah, that skunk." He said, "Yeah boy, she can retrieve, can't she?" Well, I mean he had put the sale on me. We finally got up there, and the dog came closer and was trying to deliver that pole cat to him, and Mr. Furr said, "Betty, drop that skunk!"

And when Betty didn't do it, he said again "Betty, I said drop that skunk!" Then that good ole Baptist Preacher got tested like the rest of us. He said "Betty, drop that damned skunk!" Evidently the Lord intervened before the preacher could sin anymore, and Betty did drop that skunk. We run on up that hill, and she jumped in the dog box, and we took her home. I said "Well mister, I think that's a mighty fine bird dog, and I'd like to buy her. But I swear she stinks too bad, and I can't take her home in my wife's car like that." He said "Son, don't you know nothing about pole cats."

Tomato juice will get out the odor; tomatoes will kill skunk odor in no time. So we took that dog with us as we walked to the shed, where he had canned up several quarts of tomatoes and tomato juice that previous summer. By looking in his pantry it I guessed he had over four hundred gallons of tomato juice. So we started pulling tomato juice out of the pantry and washing that dog, and all I could tell was we made the tomato juice stink, made the dog wet, made a mess on the floor, made Mr. Furr stink, and made me stink too. Here was a man trying so hard to sell a bird dog when what he really needed was to get cleaned up to go to church: I sure would love to know what his congregation thought that day when he walked in the church, cause I'm sure they could smell him.

Well, I bought that bird dog and put her in the boot (trunk) of my wife's Monte Carlo, and I headed back to Dunn. I slipped on out to Momma and Daddy's where the bird dog pen was, and I put Betty in there. My gosh, that dog still stunk, and that trunk was awful. I didn't know how to tell my bride that her car smelled so bad, so I Lysoled it, Cloroxed it, lemon juiced it, tomato juiced it, vacuumed it, and rubbed the inside of the trunk dry. When I took the car home, I didn't say anything to her about Betty or the pole cat. The next morning, she went out to get in her car, and came right back into the house, redder than a baboon's butt: "Hey! What have you done to my car?" I said, "Oh, the smell?" I cleaned that up." She retorted back, "The heck you have. Get your tail out there and fix that."

We worked on it and worked on it but there was no fixing it. Back in those days ole George Carroll was my buddy, and he owned the Chevrolet place in Dunn; I called him up and said I got this car that Sue just don't like too much anymore, so he said bring it in and we'll make a trade. I took it over to him, but only after I'd washed and perfumed her down so that she didn't reek that bad unless you knew where she was coming from. Thankfully, I traded her in and took the new car home. George sold that car there in Dunn to a couple I knew, and I seen them about two years later at the grocery store. I was talking to the man who owned it, when his bride came out with some groceries, opened the trunk, and I swear I caught a whiff of pole cat two years later, and I just said "That's Betty." When he asked, "What do you mean?" I could only reply, "Well, that's just too long a story to tell."

Big Zack

Big Zack

When they dropped the tail gate on that ole rusty Chevrolet pickup with an ole plywood dog box in the bed and a chicken wire fence tacked on the end, you'd have thought a pack of beagles were probably going to come jumping out. But what came out of that rickety old dog box would dern near take your breath away. I mean it was a F.C. Pork Roll his name was Big Zack, and when he jumped to the ground and stretched and bowed his neck, he was just about mid-thigh tall, with a long, straight tail, carried a high head, and I mean he was a beautiful ric-rack pointer. Now everybody don't necessarily know what a ric-rack pointer is: it's a black-and-white pointer dog, and his self is a little bit rare. When you looked at him you could just tell that he could run forever.

His hips were tight and he would find birds for you all day and all night. I wanted to buy Zack on site real bad, but the problem was he was quite a bit of dollars, and I needed a plan before I took him home, but I thought I could put him in the breeding program and make some of my money back. The most important thing was that he was a bird dog. Now listen, God makes a lot of pointers and setters and sends them down here every day to challenge our brain and spirit. And a lot of people mess with a lot of them, but very few of them turn out to be real bird dogs. Well, Zack was one of those dedicated few from birth; just a natural, God-touched, bird-finding machine, and that was why he was so special.

I bought him and I took ole Zack out bird hunting the first day and had him running down a hedgerow in Madamasket area between the Big Pine Woods and Fairfield; he was running down a big long cut, hedgerow on one side, beans on the other, and you could see that tall, white tail flagging as he ran. He'd run about 120 yards when he slid to a stop like a quarter horse working cows: turned in midair and pointed. Well, I went over there and flushed, and he stood the flush and shot like a gentleman; he never moved a muscle. I killed two quail and sent him in the thick stuff where the birds fell to look dead. Now Big Zack went in there and hunted hard and soon came back out and brought the first bird to me fine, I mean he delivered to hand. I sent him back in there and told him to hunt dead again, and he went and hunted up the second dead bird, but he stayed in the briar thickets a right good while; finally I called and called and he came out with the bird way back in his mouth, and I could hear the bones a crunching as he was mouthing that bird some kinda hard. When he got to me he was half swallowing the nearly chewed up bird, and I had to pull it out of his mouth. I was mad and hollered at him. but he looked at me in disdain like only a pointer can and took off hunting again. Well it didn't take Ole Zack long to find another covey of birds, and I shot two more. Zack hunted these birds dead and brought the first one into hand as he should, and I was beginning to think the other chewed up bird was just an unusual situation, but when he went and found the second bird and he'd chewed up that one as well. This went on about all day. We had nine or ten covey points and had a right good sack of birds.

But every other bird that he'd bring to me he'd chewed up. I couldn't have a bird dog, particularly a five-hundred-dollar bird dog, that would chew up the customer's birds, especially with me being in the professional hunting business—that would just be a real bad thing.

So I went to see my ole buddy J, the bird dog wizard. I said "J, I got one fine bird dog, he is absolutely outstanding, he backs on sight, he finds more birds than any other dog anybody else drops down, but every other bird we kill, that son of a gun chews them up. I mean he's hard mouth bad, he nearly swallows 'em. What we gonna do?" He said, "Now Bob, we can break that dog for sure; you know it's hard to find a dog that knows how to find wild birds, so we got to break him and make him deliver like he ought to do." J then said, "Now I heard this from a friend of mine who was Indian, and it's an old injun trick—if you do it just right, we'll save that dog." I said, "Ok J, tell me what I need to do." He said, "Ok, now you're gonna have to go to the store, and you gonna have to buy you one of them Tampa Nugget Cigars." He said, "Now they got a tight, small end on them, but they are big enough around to draw good, and then you get you some of them blue diamond matches." Then he said "Now you take that bird dog out hunting, and when he goes out there and you kill a bird, and you tell him dead, you reach in your pocket and get out that cigar and light it up, and then he said you be puffing on that cigar real good. So when he brings the chewed-up bird back to you, you take that cigar and put it right in front of his nose, and you take your hand and put down there to get to that bird and you say (give) real firm-like and when you do, you take that cigar and put it out right on his nose."

I thought, wow, this seems real harsh, but I had total faith and trust in J, and being a young dog trainer at the time, I didn't think nothing else about that. So we then walked around his barn, looked at his dogs, and talked about bird hunting, pretty girls, land and such…you know, the important things bird hunters have to talk about. We chewed a little tobacco and tried to trade a few dogs, and I went on back home and could hardly wait for that weekend to come.

When Friday night arrived I was so excited as I loaded my mess up, and back to Hyde County I went. Saturday morning come daylight you could hear the birds whistling on the roost. I started marking them down in my mind as to where they might be, as I waited for the sun to get light enough to be able to see to shoot. Well when it got light, I turned ole Zack out, and away we went.

He took off in that country sniffing and snorting and looking for a bird—it didn't take him long, and he locked up tight. Old Bell, my gype yellow-and-white pointer gype came around the corner, saw Zack, and backed about seventy-five yards away. We were ready to have a good morning. I reached down in my pocket to make sure I had me one of them Tampa Nugget Cigars and also some blue diamond stick matches, cause today was the day we was gonna fix ole

Zack. So I walked up there and told him "Whoa," and flushed them birds and shot em. I said, "Dead Zack dead," touched him on the nose and he took off looking dead and he brought the first back, pretty as he could be. He turned off to get the second bird and I reached in my pocket, got out that cigar, lit her up, and got her just as cherry red as I could. I heard him in there in the honeysuckles and the cat briers and he was cutting the shine. I could hear them little bird legs cracking and crinkling and breaking. As he was coming of the woods, I said, "Here Zack here, you come in here." He came in with that bird, and all you could see was the little ole legs dangling out where he had bitten them nearly off. He got to me and I stuck my hand right in front of his mouth, and I took that cigar and jobbed it right on the end of his nose where I tried to put it out.

Well Ole Zack really put a surprise on me—I hadn't expected what was going to come next. He took that bird and blowed it out of his mouth like a bass blowing out a fake wooden devil horse. He then chomped down on my hand, I mean he bit the loving, living poop out of my hand. I hollered, and I shook my hand, and Zack run off, but I finally got him back. He had a burnt nose and I had a bad hand, but we went on bird hunting; we killed a few more, but the cigar trick had not helped any. Ole Zack was still chewing ever other bird. Anyhow, I put Ole Zack in the truck, and took him back home.

The next day I went over to J's to tell him the tale and I said, "J, I took Ole Zack bird hunting today, and I let him out, put him out there on the hedgerow, and he took off running. He hadn't run a hundred yards when he pointed a covey of birds. I got that Tampa Nugget Cigar and matches out of my pocket and followed behind him. When the birds got up and I killed two, I sent him in there, and he brought the first one back; on the way back with that second one he started chewing him up. So, I thought I'll put this thing on the end of his nose like that ole Injun said, and we'll break him for sure. Sure nuff when he came back to me that bird was chewed up and I jabbed that cigar on his nose real hard and ground it around some." Well J. had a real strange look on his face and had gotten sort of quiet. I said "What's wrong J?" He said "Bob, to be sure, I hope you you didn't really stick that cigar on the end of that dog's nose. I was just joking with you, because you shouldn't have done that—if you do, that dog's apt to bite you."

Zippy

Wesley Cobb's Bird Dog

I was about seventeen years old when I saw a listing for setter puppies for sale in the Sunday want ads in *The News* and *The Observer*. Up to that time in my life my daddy didn't have nothing but a pack of Beagles, and I thought we needed to upgrade ourselves and become bird hunters and just not rabbit chasers. So I got in my old orange Camaro and sailed on down to Clinton, searched around and talked to people, and I found Mr.Wesley.

Mr.Wesley was a tobacco auctioneer and he was just as full of Paducah as anybody you've ever seen and had a long story and could back it up. But now he did have good bird dogs, and he had three pretty setter puppies all black and white. He said "Now son, you need to buy all these puppies." So I looked at them, and having more money than I had sense, I struck up a deal with him and came home with three setter puppies. One of them was named Spot, and he was a helluva bird dog. (When he got older and he acted like his brain rotted, and he ran up every bird in four counties when you let him out. I traded him for a old shorthair gype but that's different story.) He'd sorta point birds when he was about three and hold em until you got within gun range, turn around and smile at you, and flush em. Then there was Tiny, one classy, fine little setter bitch, would back a million miles away where there was a milk jug, a cooler, a Walmart sack or anything else she seen that was white. Then there was Boy, and he was special. Now we loved Boy and I've got a picture of him hanging up over the steps going up the stairs at my house as sort of hall of honor. I also have a peg above the fireplace with the collar of the good dogs that made it, and Boy's collar hangs up on that peg. But that's not really what this story is about.

But anyhow, I took them dogs home and I worked them and worked them—didn't have much sense and didn't know what I was doing. But we did know Mr. Jay Potter down in Santee, South Carolina, and he had a man by the name of John Allen who helped him run a shooting preserve. We went down there, and we made a deal and sent him them three puppies. When they came back they was bird dogs, they pointed, they backed and half retrieved. But as I said, Boy was just heads and shoulders above the other two: he had a good temperament and he hunted all day at a good steady pace. He had a good easy trot on him, and he found birds. He found single birds, he found covies of birds, you'd drop him down with any other dog and their dog would stand behind him way more times than not. He was just sort of that kind of special dog. I hunted him many years, and I loved him as well as I've ever loved a bird dog.

But one day I got a phone call about twenty years later from my ole buddy Jay, and he said "Bob, we've got our regular annual fall trials at the Black River Hunting Club, and we'd love for you to come judge it." Well, I said "Alright, Jay for you I'll do it." I've judged a few in my life. I'm not that fond of it, but to help other folks with their bird dogs and get things going, I like to do it. So I went and judged the field trail.

They had some really fine dogs that day: they had a little pointer bitch named Achy Breaky that won't quite two years that ended up winning the open shooting dog stake. This was right after Billy Ray Cyrus made his song, so that will tell you about what time in life it was. And we judged all them dogs, and the puppies, and the derby, and we had run the bird dogs.

Then we got into the open shooting dogs group, for which you are supposed to have real first-class dogs. There were about eight or ten open shooting dogs in that contest. I went down there and found a brace of dogs ready to run and a tall, distinguished gentleman was running one of them. He had a real nice, tall, ric rack pointer that he had been running on the circuit some. And doggone if it won't Mr. Wesley—I hadn't seen him in a long, time, and we commenced talking, laughing, and joking about old times and such.

Now I thought that Mr. Wesley was right there beside Jand God when it come to bird dogs, back when I was sixteen or eighteen years old. But we were talking and Mr. Wesley said "Bob, you need to let me win this field trial today with this old dog here. Now you know that I am the man that got you started in bird dogs. And that's the truth," I said. "Yes sir, Mr. Wesley, and there is no doubt about that, if there was any way I could do it I would do it; besides I got a bone to pick with you." He said, "What in the world kinda bone you gotta pick with me"? I said, "You remember after I bought them three dogs, I ended up buying some more dogs from you over time, over a three or four year period. Well, I went down there one day and you had a lemon-and-white pointer bitch spread out backwards on the pump house. You were down there working on that dog when we got there, and you'd taken a razorblade and were feeling around that dog's stomach, and you took and cut a little nick in that stomach. You went over and gotcha a reed, and you peeled the dead stuff off of that old reed and had that pure green stuff setting down there sticking up, and you stuck that reed in that dog's stomach, and you fished around there and fished around there and you come up with a couple of tube looking things. And I watched you and you reached in your back pocket there and got out a pack of single edge razor blades and you opened up one them an old s razorblades, and I can still see you throwing the blue paper on the ground and taking off the cardboard. And you looked real good at that dog and you took that razorblade and you cut both of them tubes. And you reached in your other back pocket, and you came out with a can of purple spray, and you sprayed that little dog right good, and then you put her down on the ground and away she went. I said, "Do you remember that Mr. Wesley? You were out there spading that dog instead of spending the money going to the vet?" He said "Yeah, sure I remember that."

I said, "Well Mr. Wesley, I thought that was the way to do things. So I went home and I watched all of my dogs, and one day I had a bitch come in heat, and I said well shoot, I ain't gonna breed that bitch, I'm gonna spade her and I ain't gonna send her up to our local vet Richard' Sorrel's to be spade. I'm gonna to do it myself just like Mr. Wesley. I didn't have a pump house to put my dog on out there at the dog house, but we did have a big ole wooden spool that used to have cable on it, and we used it as a table sometimes. So I got Henry and we took that ole bitch and put her up on that thing, and I put a rope on her and muzzled her down and turned her upside, and I started fishing on her stomach. Got me a spot about like the spot you found. Went over there and cut her stomach about an inch with my razorblade. I had to have me a reed cause you told me how you peeled it off and made it sanitary, and I went and got me a reed and cut it off with my old Barlow. I trimmed it up good and got to fishing around in there, and I didn't know exactly what I was doing, but I came up with two little cord things I thought looked like what you had. So I took my razorblade and I cut both of them cords, and I and sprayed that ole dog down with purple medicine, but she hooped and hollered, so I turned her loose and away she went. I did it just like you did." And Mr. Wesley said, "Well, what in the world is the problem with that if you did it just like I did?" I said, "Mr. Wesley, the problem is three days later my dog died," and he just barrel rolled and laughed and he said, "Well son, my dog died too."

Bobby and Split Christmas Morning

Split

I woke up in the Pamlico Hilton, an old duck hunter and fisherman's dive where you could get a room for twenty bucks a night and share the fee with as many as you could get in the room. The room was appointed with three hard wooden pallets, a bare light bulb, a broke mirror up on the wall, and a bathroom behind your truck—I mean, for a duck hunter, it had all the comforts of home.

The Pamlico Hilton was located east of Bayboro, North Carolina and I was in the area for a week of diver hunting on the sound and not doing very well. I got in my Chevy Blazer and was heading East toward Hobuckon and Pamlico Point to see what was happening in the impoundments out past Indian Island when I saw Joes old country store, so I stopped in to see if I could roust out something for breakfast. The best I could do was an aged cup of coffee about as thick as Blackstrap molasses, a mountain Dew, and a Holsum Honey Bunn, plus two cans of viennies for Gus. I got to talking to the local farmers about the price of beans and corn and slipped into the conversation whether there was anyone in the area still doing commercial hunting. Immediately they all said Bernell. I got directions on how to get to Bernell's farm, about fifteen miles from the store. I made my last turn by the post office in Hobucken and drove about a mile and a half, looking for a graded, oyster-shell road that was supposed to wind itself around some lowlands and lead to Bernell's house. I found the farm, which was pretty well Dilapidated and run down and had hogs and chickens running in the yard.

I parked and got out, looking for someone, and as I walked around the smoke house I heard a swish and a thunk: two high-school-age boys were playing stretch with jack knives. Now stretch was a game I played in high school and was a takeoff from the old English game of Mulliepeg, but in the South we changed the game and the way you played; in our version, you throw your jack knife in the ground beside the foot of your opponent and if it stuck, they had to place their foot on the spot where you stuck your knife. Then they would throw their knife in the ground beside your foot, and if it stuck you placed your foot on the spot where they stuck it. Now you keep doing this until you was all stretched out and could not spread any wider. The first one to fall was the loser. Now the game these boys were playing was just like what I played, but these guys were barefoot. Now, kids chunking knives at each other's feet did not seem like a great way to spend the day, but if one was out of duck shells I guess I understand how the game got started. As I watched the boys play, I noticed how muddy and dirty they were, and I guessed that when they went to clean up, the best way to undress them would be to skin them like a catfish.

Anyway I walked up to them and interrupted the game to ask them where Bernell was, and they told me he was out in the sound putting out FCX decoys. Now in them days the FCX was a farm co-op, and they did not sell hunting supplies unless you counted corn as a hunting supply, which is what I figured Bernell was putting out. In about thirty minutes Bernell came up the canal in his net boat and pulled into the dock beside the farm. I introduced myself and told him I had cash money and wanted to go duck hunting if he knew where any ducks where and would be willing to take me. We agreed on the price for a hunt and I would meet him the next morning at 5:00 a.m. to go shoot black heads.

Once business was done, Bernell showed me around the farm, and that's when I first saw Split, a fancy English Springer Spaniel about eight months old with a raw split lower lip. He and two younger Lab pups was eating some fish guts that was thrown out, and they looked to be relishing the food as good as the time I saw three fat girls share a cupcake at the bakery. Now as I looked at Split I took a liking to him, but I had never had a spaniel before and asked Bernell if the dog was birdie. He said he didn't know as he had only had him a couple of weeks— some fancy banker guy from Charlotte had sent him as a gift to fetch ducks for him. Then Bernell said you're a duck hunter, you know I can't take no dog like that duck hunting with my hunters; they expect a Lab. Do you want to buy him? Well, we struck a deal right there, and I paid Bernell twenty-five dollars cash for Split, and I still say it was the most dog for the money I ever bought.

I got Split home, doctored him up, and started training him, and he was smart and probably had more heart than any dog I ever owned. From the first time I sent him on a water retrieve until he died, he did a flying water entrée into every body of water he saw, including mud puddles. I guess he never figured out shallow water from deep. I will never know how Split got his bottom lip ripped open, and if Bernell knew he never told, but I guess it was because Split was pure mean. I don't mean he would hurt you—he loved all people—but other male dogs did not have a chance. He would not fight a monkey, but he would attack a gorilla if he thought it was a male dog or if he thought that gorilla was going to try and get his duck.

Split turned out to be a great dove dog and fetched so many doves for us it would be shameful to tell. He was the first dog I ever saw have a heat stroke. We were dove hunting in a cotton field full of croton (dove weed found profusely in cotton before roundup) around Falcon, North Carolina, and Split picked up every dove that five hunters shot, and I saw him panting but I didn't know then a dog could have a heat stroke. Anyway, he went to fetch a dove and fell out flat on the ground, shaking and sort of having a fit. I started hollering and crying and picked him up and drove to Dunn to Dr. Sorrels as fast as I could. Soon as I got there they knew what was going on and they put him in a cold water bath, and after about thirty minutes he started regaining his bearing. The doctor put him on an IV, gave him lots of fluids, and watched him overnight. By Monday morning we were back in business and shooting doves again.

Split became famous in our group not only because he was such a relentless dead bird dog but because of all the fights he got into. I had him in South Dakota once and was getting ready to go duck hunting at about 4:00 a.m. and was in the parking lot of Lee's Motor Inn located right on the Missouri River in Chamberlin, South Dakota. I had Split on a lead and was walking him around to get some air before we loaded up to go hunting, when I ran into two drunk Yankees coming home from the bar, standing in the parking lot by their truck. They had turned out a big Golden Retriever who was running loose, and he came over to Split with his hackles all up and profiling around Split. Now from past experience I knew this was not a good idea, and I asked them to put their dog up or put him on a lead, as I didn't want their dog to get hurt. They laughed at me and told me their dog could take care of himself, and I needed to get out of their way. Now that teed me off and I thought about just knocking both of them on their butt, but I had a better idea: I said ok boys, if you think that big kaloupa can take care of himself, it's ok with me. I reached down and unsnapped the lead on Split and nearly as quick as lightning, Split jumped that Golden, Split gripped his front paw and bit down hard, then jerked his head up. When he did this he ripped that Golden's front paw in half just like you had hit it with an axe. When they separated that Golden went to hollering just like a baby; blood was gushing everywhere, and the more that Golden jumped and hollered, the more blood got all over those boys. Now you have never seen two bad-tails turn queasy so quick. They started crying and hollering that they needed a vet. They loaded up their dog and took off. I'm not sure where they went, but I loaded Split in the truck and went to the river goose hunting, and we had a good day.

Split was like a trained martial arts fighter, and he had learned the paw trick well. I know of at least two other times when he did the same thing. One time my brother-in-law had borrowed him and they were putting in the public landing in Pamlico sound, going to the Pamlico point impoundments. I was not there, but to hear the story, it was very similar to the South Dakota experience. I saw him do it one other time in Greenwood, Mississippi at a public launch area. The men in front of us had a big Lab, and they told us to lock up our dogs as their dog was bad. I asked them to put their dog on a lead but they told me to kiss them in an inappropriate place, so I turned Split loose to do his thing: it took about thirty seconds for the event to happen, and those guys jumped got in their truck and left, giving us immediate access to the launch ramp.

Split spent his life running loose on the farm. When he'd gotten older and wasn't getting around very well, he still made a visit to the pit or the swamp every day. One morning I got up and Split was not by the door, so I went to look for him, and I found him by the pit where a cur bitch was hanging out with three wild dogs. Evidently the wild dogs did not take kindly to Split's gentleman's advances on the bitch, and a large fight started. Now when Split was young, three large wild dogs would not have been much of a challenge, but age had slowed him down, and those three gave him a bad tussle. Split had killed the two smaller males, and was still locked up with the big one when I got there. I got out of the truck, broke them up, and shot that big wild dog, then took Split home and doctored him up. He was weak and had bled at lot, but I was feeding him Jack Mackerel and milk. He hung around for three days, but the wounds and his age took its toll. He was a great dog, and to this day he is the only dog I have ever had that I throw a twenty-pound sledgehammer to fetch for exercise.

Blue

Blue

Blue was one fine setter dog, as good a dog as a man could hope to ever have. He was a big ole tall, lanky, lemon-and-white dog. When he was born, he had bright blue eyes, and as he got older they got gold colored, and he looked a lot like a lion. But old Blue could find birds. I raised Blue in the mid-1980s, and North Carolina's bird population was in a deep decline. I really dreaded the day we would lose most of the birds in eastern North Carolina, and there were very few places left to take Blue hunting. I finally sold the hunting business and was trying to get my paying business back on track—it had suffered due to my absence during the years I owned Pamlico Manor, so I gave Blue to a boy named Jerry, a big pro hunter from Missouri who hunted down in Mexico. As sad as I was without Blue, he was where he wanted to be, with birds. Blue was born as a wild bird dog and should not be destined to a life in a pen or chasing some half-crippled, liberated bird on a preserve somewhere.

When Blue was about two years old, I took him down to Mexico and we was just a hunting and killing birds all day. The area in Mexico was just south of Brownsville, Texas and had long canal ditches with a little brush on both sides of them. We'd walk down those canal ditches, and they'd be birds getting up everywhere. I remember a buddy and I saw a covey get up just as we started to hunt one of those hedgerows and I said, look and watch them singles go down, and the guide just laughed at us; see in those days singles didn't make any difference. There were so many quail and they all stayed right there, down those hedgerows, and they just concentrated more and more as you drove them down to the other end. It was a continuous bird hunt all the way down. I don't know how many birds we'd find on our high day, maybe a hundred covies, but on an average find it was fifty or sixty covies. We always killed a lot of birds and old Blue of course always did his part.

This one particular day though, we were going through the grass and saw something running through the grass, and I thought it was an armadillo, but it was a dad blame skunk. Now Blue loved birds, but be he hated critters, and Blue sailed in on that skunk and caught him, shook him, and killed him, but not before the skunk was able to discharge his most mal-odorous potion, and he just stunk up old Blue something bad. We didn't have a thing to put on him, didn't have anywhere to go with him, so we put him in the dog box and went on hunting.

We'd hunted on there for about two hours, when we came up on a junction of two canals—part of our other party had been down there hunting, so they ran into us. They had a big guy with them named Jim, who he used to play pro football and was always playing pranks on people, so I thought this might be an opportunity to get back at him. He said, "Bobby, where's Ole Blue?" I said, "Jim you won't believe this but that damned dog went into a trance. You have not ever seen nothing just like that. He said, "What do you mean?" I said, "You just go there and open up the tailgate, and when that dog comes out, you go and grab him by the ears, and when you do, his eyes will roll back into his head and he starts quivering, and he'll faint like a fainting goat. It's the darnedest thing you've ever seen. I just found out when he was retrieving a crippled bird and I don't wanna mess with him anymore, so I just put him up."

Well Big Jim, not wanting to be outdone, walked around our truck like a bull in a china shop; he ran out there to the other truck that Blue was in and he dropped the tailgate. Blue wanted to come out—he didn't care that he had been skunked. Jim was so busy wanting to see this dog pass out with his eyes rolled back into the back of his head that he didn't even catch the smell to start with. He opened that tailgate and opened the dog box, Blue came out and he grabbed him by his head and started twisting his ears. The ole dog hollered, and Jim said "Bobby, that dog won't pass out—you should go ahead and hunt him." The dog hollered again, and about that time he said, "Oh my God! What in the hell is that?" By that time we all couldn't stand it: we laughed and laughed and rolled on the ground we laughed so hard.

Well, the thing about old Jim was, he was big, probably 320 pounds, and in pretty doggone, good shape, strong enough to lift a freight train, and although he liked to play pranks on everybody else, he did not take them well himself. We just sort of stayed out of his way for the rest of the day. But that night when we were all back in the cabanas and everybody had been drinking a little tequila and having a big time, people got to teasing Jim about the skunk dog, and it just gave him the red tail, sure enough. I could tell they were really getting under Jim's skin with that, and since I was the architect of this scheme, I might just need to make my exit and sneak out of there the best way I could. So I just eased into my room, closed the door, and got in bed, getting ready to go to sleep, so I would feel like getting up and going hunting early the next morning.

Well, I hadn't been in there for very long when I heard somebody knocking on my door: it was Big Jim feeling all the effects of the tequilla. "Rupert, you in there? Come on out here, I wanna talk to you." I said, "I ain't coming out there this night, Jim." He said, "You'd better get your butt out here. I wanna talk to you." I thought, he was gonna kill me and I was sitting there on my bunk bed thinking hard on how to get out of this mess, when all of a sudden ka-wham-a-wam-a-wam! He had kicked the door slap off the hinges. I said, "Oh Lord, this does not look good to me." He came sailing into that room and tried to grab a hold of me, and I had pulled up into a ball. So he grabbed the mattress and pulled the whole damn thing onto the floor, rocked the bunk bed, and it turned over sideways. Well it turned over onto him, and I jumped down on the other side and shimmed on outside like a slick goose. Then he came out behind me but I made it outside to the dark where he couldn't see all that good, I reckon, so I ducked and dodged him for a little while; then finally he calmed on down, and I came on back in and went to bed.

The moral of the story—the best I can tell—is "If you got a skunked dog, don't roll his ears."

General Hank Emerson, and Col. Bob Rupert my father in Chamberlin South Dakota 1980

Pinewoods Bird Dog

Well, I went out one day with my buddy J, and we were gonna bird hunt in the big ole flat, tall pinewoods in Sampson County. He had a couple of pretty nice standing pointers, and I had Boy. Now Boy was the best setter God ever graced me with, unless you consider Blue. He was a big black-and-white setter with lots of bottom, and I also had Ole Slab, a fine ole big liver-and-white pointer. Big ole broad head, big wide nose—he was a bird machine. Well, we were bird hunting that morning somewhere between Dunn and Piney Green, and we found a right smart of birds. We sorta snuck in them ole flat pine lands owned by the timber company and was doing right good. We heard a chain saw running in there, which was unusual, cause this was posted land. We hunted on and ended up on a log trail close to the man cutting wood, and who was it but old Cephus.

He was cutting firewood and putting it on an ole truck and trailer and hauling all the firewood to the house. You should have seen that trailer with its bald tires sorta angled outward cause it carried such a load of wood. We stopped and talked to Cephus—Jknew him pretty well, but I just sort knew him in passing. He had a pack of beagles tied up on the backside of that trailer and the ugliest, scroungiest old bird dog you've ever seen. She was a gype pointer, liver and white, with spots of hair missing in several places, and the rest of her hair thin and dull. We were just sitting there talking and enjoying a break and passing time. We had a little bit of cheese and viennies and a square nab and a Pepsi. We shared with Cephus and got to talking about hunting, mostly rabbit and bird hunting, and a little about coon hunting, and Jlooked up at Cephus and said, "Hey, Cephus, what about that old bird dog you got?" He said "Ain't no count Mr. J, sorriest thing I've ever seen. She want run no rabbit with the pack, no sir—she wont open up with them when they hit a trailthat dog just scares me to death. Say I take her out here with these beagles and I turn her a loose: she just runs the other way, and I goes and looks for her and she is on point. All that dog do is point birds and point birds and they get up and "brrrrrr"—scare me to death. I just don't think nothing of her. Now she'll scare you to death pointing birds and pointing birds…I can't kill no birds, no how. She ain't worth a flip."

Jay said, "Why don't you let us hunt her this afternoon, and we'll meet you back here. If she points any birds, I"ll buy her." He said, "You just do that Mr. J. Remember, ole Cephus said she ain't no good ain't no count at tal. Just do what you wanna do." So here we were with four high-powered bird dogs and a scroungy, flea-bitten, broken-down, liver-and-white pointer bitch. I thought now ain't this a heck of a mess. I said, "I sure hope nobody sees us J." "Well, them four high-powered, big-time bird dogs run by a bamboo briar thicket, and that that ole pointer bitch of Cephus's whose name was Sally had slipped down there and pointed right at the edge of a small drainage ditch where it run out of the bean field back toward the briar thicket. Now them other dogs had passed them birds, but I hollered and they came back around and backed as they should, and we got up there and flushed a nice covey of birds. Killed four birds and Sally went right in there and retrieved every one of them birds.

Well, that story went on all day long, we got seven covies and she pointed every one of the them. Every one of them high powered dogs was up behind her every time, and she retrieved most of them. She was ugly on point with a low tail and had her belly nearly on the ground, but that bitch was one-time bird machine. She'd find every bird around plus some of their cousins that hadn't even been born yet.

That afternoon we eased on back to where we'd left Cephus with that scrounge pack of hounds, and J was going to have buy Sally. I mean she was ugly as she could be, but she was a bird machine. So he got ready and said to Cephus, "Now Cephus, I got this old dog, and I agree she ain't much count, but I believe that I'll buy her and take her on home since it is nearly Christmas, and you and Aunt Maggie could use a little money—I can work with her and make her into a little something and should be able to sell her to somebody." Now Cephus had been trading dogs nearly as long as J, and he could tell he had J lathered up, and all he needed to do now was shave him. Cephus said, "Now you know Mr. J, that's a right smart good bird dog now." J old Cephus knows a good bird dog when he sees one and said, "I gotta have two hundred dollars." Well, I can tell you what Jay couldn't reach in his pocket fast enough to give that man two hundred dollars.

J thought early on in the day he was going to buy Sally for twenty dollars, but that was one fine dog, and J could not risk losing her for only $180. Now in J's kennels, there was a special pen of honor where he always kept his personal dogs that he would not sell and that is where old Sally stayed the rest of her life. Sally had no papers, no nothing: more important than that she was a bird dog.

The Big Shot

It was an early morning on opening day of quail season 1985 when I pulled up in the yard of J's house about 5:30 in the morning. There were old pickups scattered all around, including my old Chevy. When I got out of my car and went on in the house, you could smell country ham frying...gaa-lee did it smell good with them biscuits coming out of the oven, right hot, plus grits, red-eye gravy, and plenty of eggs and homemade pear preserves. That's what Aunt Robena was famous for. They was just as good as you could ever eat.

Any rate there was J and three other guys, and one of them had a new pick up with a metal dog box. I ain't never seen no aluminum dog box before—we'd always built ours out of scrap lumber and chicken wire—but this guy had one. I got to looking on the front of his truck, and his tag said Raleigh. I mean he had come from Raleigh all the way to Dunn, North Carolina, to go bird hunting with us, and we was going to drive all the way to the Sandhills.

Anyhow, we got to eating breakfast, and Jay introduced him to Sambo, Ralph, and me. We all said, "Hi" and started talking birds and dogs. Now five people is a plenty to go bird hunting, but no one broke off cause all of us wanted to see who had the best dogs. See, the winner could have bragging rights all the way back home and talk lots of junk until the next hunt. We all had three or four dogs, and the city man who happened to be a banker had on his brand new Filson britches, plaid starched shirt, and hadn't never seen no mud or briars on none of his attire. And he had with him one of them humpback Browning Sweet 16 shotguns, and I mean it was a pretty thing, brand sparkling new and didn't have nar a bit of rust on it. My ole Remington 58 had sort of a patina rust cover all across it and cut down to Cylinder Bore by me and D.B. in the shop with a hack saw. But nonetheless, we was talking bird dogs and eating breakfast, and just shoveling it in and having a time. And J was talking 'bout taking Red and Sally, and the city feller said, "Well I hope your dogs is broke. Cause I don't like to go with people whose dogs ain't broke." And J, he said "You mean a dog that points birds and backs and hunts dead and retrieve dead birds." He said "Yes, that's exactly what I mean." "Honor my point," J said. "What do you mean, 'honor your point'?" "Shine your dogs might not even point a bird." He said "Son, I have two of the highest professional trained pointers that has ever been in North Carolina. They are not only pointers they are steady to wing and shot, they can point a quail from a hundred yards." JW said, "Well look here man, I don't know about that, but I can't shoot a bird at a hundred yards. I don't need one that can point that far. I need my dog to get up there a little bit closer in shotgun range." J then said "I'll tell you what, you go ahead and let them big-time dogs out, and I'll let mine out, and we'll just make a deal. If mine runs er a bird up, you just shoot him and kill him right then and that will be alright with me, and I'll never say a word. But I want you to know that if yours runs er a bird up, I aim to shoot him too."

Well things sorta got right quiet, and we all got into two pickups and loaded up and headed on to the Sandhills for the big opening day. We got there at the Sandhills, and the first head we let out to hunt had a bunch of little ole Scrub Oaks and bean fields on the edges, and some of the beans had just been picked, but most of them was still standing in the field. And we started to turn the dogs out: J turned out a dog, Sambo turned out a dog, and I turned out Blue, a fine belton lemon-and-white setter with gold eyes, which had been blue when he was a pup, and we said, "Come on city fella, are you gonna turn out a dog or what?" He said, "I'm not gonna turn out one of mine here…this place doesn't look right to me." So we went on and hunted that spot. J's ole red dog got on down there around the edge first and froze up like a statue, and all the other dogs coming around that edge saw him and backed like they was supposed to, and we went in there and shot some birds. We killed four or five birds on the covey rise, and the dogs picked em up pretty quick and went on down the field to a reed bed to try and find some singles, and everything was going along pretty good. We had some good dog work and pointed several singles and mostly just shot the Bob's and let the hens go.

Then we decided to quit and let the rest of the birds go for seed, so we loaded up and decided to go on to another head. This next place was more opened up— Pinewoods you could walk in—so we let out a bunch of dogs, several big runners. I let out two, Jay let out two, and

Sam let out two, and we asked the city feller if he was going to let out them big running pointers as this was good place for them, and he said, "I don't believe I'm gonna let mine out right here."

So any rate, we went on and walked them pine flats. We got a few birds and got them scattered out there and found some singles and had a pretty good shoot. Got to be time for us to come out of there; it was lunch so we stopped out at the store and got some potted meat and Vienna's and crackers. I think somebody got a box of smoked sausage and a slab of cheese, and we all got a Pepsi Cola and maybe put some peanuts in it and something like that—I think Sambo even got a pig foot. But we all had lunch, sat there, and ate and talked about our hunting, who shot what, who missed what, which went on about an hour or so, until about 2:30 that afternoon we decided we were gonna let them out again. So we pulled up to this real pretty broom straw field that had some feed plots with peas and lespedeza planted in there. I had a couple of young dogs that hadn't hunted yet, so I thought I'd let them out. We were ready to see them big-time, professionally trained pointer dogs that the city feller had from Raleigh. So we got out there and turned our dogs loose, and J turned out a young setter gype, and Sambo turned out a rangy ric-rack pointer dog and told the city feller, now go ahead and turn yurn out cause we ready to see them big-time dogs. "Well my dogs ah, I don't put them in a broom straw field, cause stuff gets up their nose."

Well, any rate we bird hunted all day; by the time we come back home that city feller never did turn them dogs out. I don't know why he brung em, I don't know what was going on, but there was something funny about it. He never did, turn them dogs out. We were riding back and I said to J, after pondering everything. "J, what in the world do you reckon was wrong with that city feller to bring all them dogs all the way from Raleigh and then drag them all the way from there to the Sandhill's; he talked such a big show, but he never would turn them loose." J said "Well son, it was a lack of confidence. He just didn't have no confidence in his bird dogs."

Top Three

The alarm clock was ringing rudely, when I dragged my butt out of bed at quarter till three on a cold, brisk January morning, with the wind blowing about fifteen miles per hour and a overcast sky threatening to rain. I got on the phone and called the boys to make sure they were up. We were going to meet up at Fred Tew's Store parking lot at 3:15 a.m. and would be heading out to the coast to go duck hunting.

On this particular day we were going out with Roland Stiener to the banks on Core Sound. Roland lived in the Harker's Island area. If you don't know where I mean, it's out there past Algie Willis Ferry landing. Anyhow, I picked up Rob and Steve, got them in the truck, and off we went just as fast as we could. We went through Newton Grove and got into Kinston 'bout quarter till five.

Back in those days, the Neuse Sports Shop had a grill open in the back. Took them boys in there and they got them a bologna, egg, and cheese sandwich. On the way out we picked up some potted meat, crackers, Vienna sausage, pickled pigs feet, dill pickles, some hoop cheese, sunflower seeds, Redman Chewing Tobacco, and a case of Mountain Dew.

We got on down there, met Mr. Rowland, got in the boat, and headed out across the sound just at daylight. Roland had already spread the decoys out pretty good. As we crossed the sound, we could see large rafts of bluebills, some of which had already started trading the shoreline, looking for breakfast We were excited by seeing so many ducks and knew that our chances were getting better as we were hoping to try and kill a few blue bills, redheads, and maybe a Canvasback now and then. I ain't so sure that at the particular time Canvasbacks were legal: very likely they won't, but we would have probably shot one if he had come in. I have no idea if we killed any or not, can't remember.

Well, we were out there that morning, and the boys kept eating that poggie bait and all that junk we purchased from Neuse Sport

Shop. It was a sort of cloudy, low ceiling morning, holding everything down, especially hot air from conversation and other parts of the human anatomy. That ole Steven boy cut one, and I mean it come up there, blowed up his wadders like a balloon at the state fair. Now the vapors were just easing out of the top of his wadders, and I mean I thought that boy was gonna die of his own vices. I mean it was a smelling, sure enough bad, it was wretched; it was so bad, it would gag a maggot. But nonetheless, we got through it. They were sitting there saying that must have been the worse fart of all time. "What do you think, Uncle Bobby?" I said, "No boys, that might be bad, but it ain't even in the top three." That cloud of stench hanging low over our heads had us hanging our head out of the blind trying to get some fresh air. They said, "Well, tell us about the top three then." I said, "Ok, but those three are just so far ahead of that fart that you'll never know."

Well, number three on the list is the bait house dump. See back a few years ago we had gone croaker fishing down in the Chesapeake Bay near downtown Newport News at the James River. We had been out there all day, eating all that kind of mess and all that junk, 'bout like these boys were just eating. When we come in for lunch, one of the ole boys fishing with us, he couldn't stand it, he was about to bust to take a dump. We were in the bait house getting more bait, drinks, and ice and that kind of stuff. We smelled right rough from cutting up all that shrimp and fish all day out there in the sound in the heat. Well, the boy with us could not wait—he had to go right there and hit that man's toilet…I mean he blowed the bottom slap off of it, with all the grunting and groaning and everything, we weren't sure just what was going to happen. When that boy came out of there, he had sort of a green look. That odor that followed him, I mean eeewwwweeee, it turned your belly—rolled it upside down and back. Folks coming in the bait shop were holding their noses and thought that man was selling rotten fish and bad bait cause I'm telling you that place stunk, and when you can stink up a bait house, you're doing pretty good. Now that's number three on the all-time list.

Number two is "Wino Roses." See a group of us were traveling down to Florida one day, going towards Clewiston. We were going to go bass fishing out there on the lake. It seems like every time I get into these malodourous events, it's in a hunting and fishing environment. Seems most of the guys drank liquor and ate pickled eggs and hoop cheese, liver pudding, souse meat and such as that for the entire trip. That's sort of what happened on this one. After about four hours on the road, we pulled into a convenience store to get some gas, as we were dead on empty. KP was in the back and he got out to go to the toilet, had to go bad. He got to the bathroom door, but there was a crippled man in there, so KP could not get inside so he waited and danced and moved his legs back and forth. Well, finally, the crippled man came out and KP got in. With all the growling and grunting going on, you would have thought there were two bears a fighting back in there, or wild beast mating, or some such thing as that. I mean, there was a terrible noise going on.

Well, while he was in there, a wino came in, and he had to go to the bathroom, I spoke to him and said "How are you doing?" He said, "I'm ok, had a bad night; I got just enough money to buy one beer to get me over this hangover." So he's waiting to get in there, to the toilet, standing there about the time KP came out with a lighter step in his gate. And that wino opened that door—I'm talking about a man who looked bad. I mean this is a man who had been drunk for a month, He had just come from being wine drunk, and that's a tough one. He walked into that toilet, and the door had no more closed on his butt when he come out there with tears running down his face, his nose flared, and he was a gagging. He walked right up there to the counter, and I don't know if you remember, but a lot of convenience stores used to sell scented paper roses. He grabbed that flower and started smelling that rose, bringing it back and forth across his nose, gasping for air. He told the woman he had to buy that rose and gave her his last $1.35. As he was walking out the door he said, "What did I ever do to deserve that?" Now any fart that can turn a wino to a flower lover is strong.

So those are the top two and three of my noxious experiences, but neither of them is close to number one. The most noxious tale I can tell you, the most malodorous of all is the Hoyt Paralyzer. I met Hoyt on an Antelope hunting trip right off the Moose Thompson Ranch in Wyoming. He comes from somewhere down in South Carolina, down there past Orangeburg, and I'm thinking somewhere in Denmark or Sweden or one of them little spots named after a European country. He owned a couple of trailer parks, and was a pretty good hunter and a good guy. I'm sure he's rotted from the inside out by now because that was one stinking man. You see, we had Hoyt, myself, and three other guys in the backseat of the suburban. We were out there antelope hunting and going from one spot to another. We were driving down the highway, looking for places to hunt, when Hoyt had a terrible run of gas. When those noxious fumes started coming out of his bowels, they made a yellow cloud just like tear gas or something filling up in that truck. I had to stop the car—rolling down the windows won't enough—and we had to jump out; there were five men out there in freezing weather in their shirt sleeves, trying to get outside of that noxious cloud to get some fresh air, so they could breathe. I'm telling ya'll this thing was so bad, there was a tractor trailer coming up the highway, and when he went through that yellow cloud he started swerving: I thought he was going to turn over on a straight highway. He finally got that truck stopped, and he got out gasping for air. Now any man that can cut a fart that is so prolific that he can stop a tractor trailer going down the highway has got to be the all-time farter if there ever was one.

Jackson and Jeb

Tuffy

It was an early December morning, and pretty cold, when I went over to Falcon. I met Bruce just as I passed the Black River bridge, and we went on to downtown Falcon, then down about a mile from there to a little old swamp head. They tended the cotton on one side of the head, and somebody else tended the land on the other side. On one end was an old farm house, where there lived a man, who I've always heard was a little bit queer, but I've never had no run-ins with him. Anyhow, we started through the reed bank, and the birds got up real spooky. We didn't get a point, didn't get a shot.

We kept hunting that morning, and the further we went up the branch, the more birds keep geeting up spooky and we ain't killed no birds, and the dogs hadn't done bad, hadn't run nothing up. Anyhow, we got on down back to the end, and we got a point; we were walking to the point, when a cat run out of them bushes and right up top of a tree. 'Bout that time the birds got up and we shot at them. I heard BOOM

BOOM from Bruce, and he had killed a bird on the left and shot that cat in the tree. But, that cat didn't fall out. I shot a bird too and stomped on through there and looked for him, and I seen Bruce take off running. I thought that was awfully funny thing for him to take off running like that, and about that time I heard him yell, "RUN! RUN! Mr. Jones! Mr. Jones!" And I thought well, there's that guy…he must have been mad as hell that we were bird hunting, I reckon. Anyhow, he come up and he had me caught right there in the middle of the bean field, and I couldn't get away from him, as Bruce had already gone to the other side of the branch and was gone. He was tearing me up one side and down the other. I said "What'd we do?" He said, "You shot my house." There was a shot when we shot up in the air raining down on top of his roof, and that pissed him off, royal. He was as mad as a wet, sitting hen, and he kept talking trash to me about trespassing and poaching, how he was gonna kill me, and sue me, and take me to the law and all that stuff. Meanwhile, all I was looking for was a hole, where I could get away.

About the time he was really getting into the middle of his tirade, you heard the dangest squall up there in that tree: "rawaaww!" The cat hollered up in that tree, and he was hanging on by one claw, the one that Bruce had shot. He squalled out again, and as he fell that man said, "TUFFY!" And he had run over there as fast as he could to get his cat, and when he left me in just a little bit of daylight, I could tell right then he sorta liked that cat. And there won't no need in me sitting there talking to him about it, so I hauled tail, and when I got on the other side of the branch, and Bruce picked me up.

We loaded up the dogs and headed our way out of Falcon. There I was sitting there, recollecting about what all had happened, and I said I reckon you got a double: you shot the man's house and you shot the man's cat. Anyway we laid low from that area and didn't bird hunt there for at least two more years. I understood the old man moved off, and after he got gone we started hunting in that head again.

Bobby, Cody and Sidney in Mingo Swamp

Wild Goose Chase

We had a party/blind pull every hunting morning from an old shoe box at the Pamlico Manor Hunting Lodge I had back in the 80s. It was my turn, and I got to guide two bankers from Winston Salem, and I ain't always been particularly fond of bankers, no how. They dressed like Ted Williams and had fancy shotguns, though they didn't hardly know which end to load them from and couldn't shoot a bull in a barrel. Nonetheless I drew the Green Hill Blind, and it was a good spot: I had had the whole family down there duck hunting for a day just the week before.

We pulled in there about 5:30 a.m. It was pitch dark, and we put our waders on. It was unusually cold, and the impoundment still had some ice on the edges as we went in, so it was a little bit slippery. We got out there to the area we were to hunt, and we had a really nice blind. I got the guys in there, and got them set down and covered up. They had their coffee cups with them and that was fine. I set the decoys in a fine J spread and everything was good. Just before break of day you could start hearing ducks and geese flying everywhere. I mean it looked like it was going to be one of those days, just a little light wind, maybe five to ten miles per hour coming out of the east.

When the sun was just coming up, there seemed to be birds everywhere. Just as the boys were finishing their coffee, a flock of Teal came in. Them boys commenced shooting when I told them to take em, and when they did, the dadblamdest noise came out of the bulrushes back there about two hundred yards behind us. They said, "What is that?" I said, "Gah, I ain't sure never heard nothing in my life like that…dadbladest noise I ever heard. I don't know what that was." Well, those guys got sorta quiet—acted like they were scared. Two or three minutes later another flock of ducks come in and we shot again, and that noise happened again, except it was just a little bit longer this time than it was the time before. Again they asked, "What in the world is that?" "I told you, I ain't got no idea what that is."

About that time another flock of ducks come in, and we shot them and got a couple of Gadwall and a black. I walked out there to help give the dog a line in picking up the ducks. Gus my old yellow Lab was out there picking up the ducks when we heard that noise back there in the bushes again. So I decided there was no way for us to figure out what was going on unless we went to see, so I spoke to them boys and said "I'm going to go over there and see what's making such a fuss." They said, "What do you think it is?" I said, "I don't know—maybe a bear…probably not, but give me my gun just in case. I'll just go over there and find out what it is."

Well, I eased out into the water and in that direction it was mucky, and I was slipping up to about my knees on every step I'd pull; and I'd walk, and I'd get hot, and I'd cuss; I'd pull, and I'd walk, and I'd cuss, and I'd get hot. Finally, I made it over about to the edge of a wind row in the middle of the impoundment. And as I got closer, that noise took off in high gear and the dadblamest shaking and rattling and stuff was going on. Like it was trying to get away from me a little bit, but it wasn't getting that far. Well, I got over to that hedgerow and got to looking, and I could see a ripple in that water way back in there, and there was something moving around. It was too thick for me to get further back in, so I moved slowly back though the tangled bushes and called old Gus and sent him in. He charged in that tangle and got to chasing something, and doggone if he didn't come up with a goose. It seems that some of them other boys from the Manor had been hunting, and instead of putting up their decoys when they finished hunting, they had put about twenty or thirty decoys in a wad in there. And evidently this goose had come in there and was a feeding right on the edge of the hedgerow and got his feet and wings hung up in them decoy cords. He was in a mess, all wrapped up in decoy cord and could not get away; all he could do was beat his wings and holler. He was a beating those bushes and reeds with his wings, and he just made an unearthly racket.

Well, I finally got that ole goose, grabbed him up, and held him by the wings. It took me several minutes to get the strings off his feet and toes, and off his legs, wings and nose, but nonetheless I finally got him loose and walked back over there, holding him by the wings. He was just cutting the shine. Nonetheless, I had him, and I got him back over to the boys and climbed back into the blind. We were sitting there, and they had killed a few ducks, but they hadn't killed any geese.

One of them boys said, "Throw that goose up." "What do you mean throw him up?" I asked. And he said, "throw him up high in the air, we gonna shoot him." I said, "This goose is in the blind; let's just ring his neck and put him in the bag." He said, "Naw, we are gonna shoot him." I said, "All right." So I heaved him up there and throwed that goose up in the air, and that ole goose said ga-honk, ga-honk and started to fly. The boy on the left went ba-boom, ba-boom, ba-boom, and the guy on the right went ba-boom, ba-boom, ba-boom. The boys where shooting, and the goose went ga-honk, ga-honk. On the left, ba-boom, ba-boom, ba-boom, on the right, ba-boom, ba-boom, ba-boom, ga-honk, ga-honk. Slowly that goose gained altitude, and they shot another time or two, ga-honk, ga-honk, and for the next two hundred yards the goose got smaller, and the noise got quieter, ga-honk, ga-honk, and he flew out of sight. Those two guys sat there looking at each another, sort of stupid, and they turned on me like a rattlesnake: "You throwed him up too high." So I guess you get the idea of what it's like to be a guide.

Blue Pointing, Zack backing Hyde County

Good-Bye Mr. Bob

I drove my old pickup to the back of the cul-de-sac. The cul-de-sac is not some fancy housing development in the suburbs, it's a tear-shaped field at the end of my farm, long and narrow with a hook off to the west.

That's where I got out to pay tribute and send my respects to Mr. Bob. You see that old cul-de-sac is the last place I seen him, and all these years later I come back here at the first of March just to be able to pay my respects to Mr. Bob.

Mr. Bob had both a major impact on Southern culture as a whole and as a single entity on my own life. You could go to church, and when the service was over, everybody would be on that big porch talking and visiting, and inevitably two or three conversations would come up about Mr. Bob. For Mr. Bob was a major influence not only on our Southern culture, he was part of our life and moral fiber.

You see, growing up with Mr. Bob taught boys how to become a gentleman. He taught us sharing, humility, pride, and civic responsibility In addition to being a tutor for so many young men, he was also a major industrial player, spawning varied industries from clothing, real estate, horse and wagons, saddlery, dog paraphernalia, kennels, books, and recipes. In fact he had a major impact on all the industries of the south for many decades. But Mr. Bob, he wasn't some legend or tale or even a famous man: Mr. Bob was simply Bobwhite Quail.

People that has never had the privilege of stomping through the woods and swamps in search of Mr. Bob has really never had the opportunity to live or hunt. Oh I know, the guys that have chased elk and heard a bugle have_had a wonderful experience, or maybe a select few that have heard a lion roar in Africa, that was for sure a bone-chilling experience. But see, as great as other wildlife experiences can be, none of that compares to a wild covey flush of Mr. Bob's, as you are tangled up in some bamboo briars, stepping across a ditch of honeysuckles vines, as you're headed into a broom straw field and have Mr. Bob abrupt under your feet—your heart comes to your throat, and it's absolutely the world's largest thrill. To see a big pointer dog running across a bean field headed to the end of the hedgerow and freeze in midair, his head held high, his tail erect, his nose quivering, and his whole body in a tremble, all standing in honor of Mr. Bob is sure a site to behold, one of the greatest sporting sites ever.

Backed up at most Southern churches, every truck had a dog box, and in that dog box was war battered, worn pointers and setters, their ears ragged and scratched. Their noses showed the lines of a million cat briars that had cut them over the days, ears shredded in fine strings like twine. Their tails were raw for the first four inches, some of them were scabbed or nubbed or stubbed over where they fell off after so many years of chasing Mr. Bob.

My mom could take an old quail, brown him in a frying pan, pour in some milk and flour, and make gravy, then let him simmer with the lid on. Make up a pan of rice and buttermilk biscuits. Nothing ever ate no finer than Mr. Bob.

L.L. Bean, Stillson, Gander Mountain, Hearders: these names are old sporting retail companies, all owing part of their success to Mr. Bob too. Then Remington, Peters, L.L. Smith, Browning, particularly the humpback Sweet 16, Remington 1148, 58 and later the 1100, Parkers, 00 Framed 20s, 28s, 410s, Winchester 21s, Fox

Speciality Grade, Idea Grade, L.C. Smith Ideal grade, Parker's Trogan through A1 Specials—a total industry of guns made around Mr. Bob.

Other companies included Scout International trucks and Jeeps, for Mr. Bob had a major impact on those vehicles as well. His reach extended to real estate, cook books, how-to books, dog training books, Elhue Kennels, and Peters Old Blue shotgun shells, all supportive of Mr. Bob.

I was lucky enough to grow up chasing Mr. Bob: it was such a wonderful opportunity that my children never really got to experience. Today, I raise wonderful Labradors and great dogs they are; I enjoy going to the swamps shooting Mallard, Teal, Wood Ducks, an occasional goose, but none of that provides the thrill of the covey eruption with Mr. Bob. It brought us comradeship, it taught us the gentleness, it showed us a graciousness, and how to share: you shoot the ones on the left, and I'll shoot the ones on the right. I'll wait for you, your dog will honor mine, my dog will honor yours, we'll honor each other. What a better moral and civil society we lived in due to Mr. Bob. Today, these kids run around with their britches pulled down, cracks showing, drawers hanging out, tattoos—my God all over everywhere—plugs in their ears, studs in their lips, and things in their nose and their ears. This just won't the way it was supposed to go with men, or was it with a time with Mr. Bob.

So every year I'll make my heritage down there to the cul-de-sac, where I can still see that covey running across that bean field. I still remember them getting up that last covey, only six birds, four hens, and two Bob's. I sat there and pulled my gun up on them but couldn't shoot, it was so rare to see. I said "Bang, Bang" and then "Good bye Mr. Bob." I am so thankful I was able to grow up Southern and to have known Mr. Bob.